THE SURPRISE

For Katherine, Harvey & Maud —Z. S. & N. L.

For my mum, Angela. And my oddball, Joel. —M. F.

VIKING
An imprint of Penguin Random House LLC, New York

First published in the UK by Penguin Books Ltd., 2021
This edition published in the United States of America by Viking,
an imprint of Penguin Random House LLC, 2022

Visit us online at penguinrandomhouse.com.

Library of Congress Cataloging-in-Publication Data is available.

Manufactured in China

ISBN 9780593525975

10 9 8 7 6 5 4 3 2 1

HH

Text set in Bohemia LT Std

ZADIE SMITH   NICK LAIRD

THE SURPRISE

illustrated by
MAGENTA FOX

VIKING

It was Kit's birthday.

Her present was a soft, small, sleepy surprise.

She's perfect! Kit whispered.
But why's she dressed like that?

No one knew.
The Surprise wasn't telling.

Kit left for school. The Surprise woke up.

She was surrounded.

But what is it?
chirped Paul.
She clearly can't fly.

Not a cat. Too round,
said Dora.

Or a pug, Bob decided.
Those legs!

She don't do much, noted Paul.
Actually, whispered the Surprise,
    I'm quite into judo, Paul.

What's that now? barked Bob.
He was a bit deaf.

She just said she's an oddball, sniggered Dora.

Are you an oddball? asked Bob.
The Surprise didn't know what to say.

Oh, she's definitely an oddball,
said Dora. *If you're not a cat
or a dog or a bird, you're an oddball.*

According to the schedule, Bob announced,
it is now time to watch Animal World.
Do you watch Animal World? asked Paul. It's on
the schedule.

I've only seen the judo, Paul,
whispered the Surprise.

She said she's always been an oddball! shouted Dora, and with that,
Dora and Bob padded into the living room to watch telly,
with Paul fluttering after.

The Surprise was left alone.

She thought about ways to make herself more like the others.

She sat down and felt sad.

Then she had an idea.

SURPRISE!

shouted the Surprise,
I can fly.

But just then,
a gust of wind came in
one window . . .

and blew the Surprise out the other.

Oops, she thought.

The Surprise was worried. Maybe she was going to
go into the clouds. Or up into forever overhead.

But just as she was floating past the last balcony,
when all seemed lost . . .

. . . she met somebody.

Hello, said the somebody, I'm Emily Brookstein.
And what's your name?
Everyone calls me Oddball, said the Surprise.

Oh, they call me odd, too, said Emily Brookstein.
Life's too short not to be an oddball.
Why do they think you're odd?

I think, said the Surprise,
because I am unaware of the schedule.

Heaven save us from schedules! cried Emily,
and brought out a plate of coconut macaroons.

Now what's your real name?

I don't know. I'm Kit's
birthday present.

Are you indeed!
Well, I had an Aunt Melody
who looked a bit like you.
She was an oddball.
Kept boiled eggs in her pocket
and stayed out dancing ever so late.

Oh.

The Surprise and Emily Brookstein
played cards

and ate macaroons

until the grandfather clock
struck three.

Emily said,
*I wish you could stay all day,
but it must be about time
to take you back. Your Kit
will be getting home soon.*

When Kit saw the Surprise, she gave her
a very long and very nice hug.

And the Surprise thought,
    Oh, that's what I do. I get hugged.

You guys . . . said Kit. Meet Maud.

Maud, is it? murmured Bob,
who could hear perfectly
well when he wanted to.

*We were only a bit mean because we were
worried you might be an oddball,*
said Dora.

Maud smiled and thought of Emily.
*I **am** an oddball, she said. But I am also a Maud.*

Sorry about earlier, said Paul.
Can you by any chance teach us some judo?

So they added judo to the schedule.